All inquiries should be addressed to:
Barron's Educational Series, Inc.
250 Wireless Boulevard
Hauppauge, New York 11788
http://www.barronseduc.com

ISBN-13: 978-0-7641-5231-3
ISBN-10: 0-7641-5231-9

Library of Congress Catalog Card No. 00-100808

Manufactured by: M03103D, Guangdong, China
Manufactured date: January 2012
39 38 37 36 35 34 33 32 31

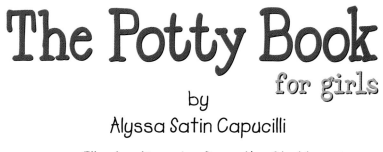

The Potty Book
for girls

by
Alyssa Satin Capucilli

Illustrations by Dorothy Stott

BARRON'S

Hello! My name is Hannah.
I have lots of fun each day.

But first I need my diaper
changed, so I can go and play.

I can eat *my* breakfast by *myself*.
I can brush *my* teeth at the sink.

I can choose the clothes I want to wear.
I really love hot pink!

Mommy has a big, big box,
she says it's just for me.
Daddy helps me open it,
whatever can it be?

Is it a brand new fish bowl?
No, it couldn't be!

Maybe it's a big, big boat
to sail across the sea!

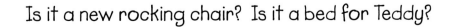

Is it a new rocking chair? Is it a bed for Teddy?

Mom says it's my very own potty,
to use when I am ready.

I look down at my diaper.
It seems to fit just right.
My diaper's where I pee and poop,
morning, noon, and night.

Mom and Dad use a potty, maybe I will try.
If I can use my potty, then my pants will stay dry!

I sit on my very own potty.
Teddy sits with me.

Off goes my diaper,
when I want to poop or pee.

Some days I hurry to the potty.
Woops! I am too late!

Some days I sit and read a book. . .

. . . or sing a song as I wait!

Uh-oh! I had an accident!
My pants are very wet.
Mom and Dad say, "That's okay, Hannah.
Don't you give up yet!"

Then one morning I wake up,
and whisper to my Teddy,

I'm off to the potty,
I think this time I'm ready!

Off goes my diaper,

Teddy sits on my lap,

I wait a bit...

I look inside...
and then I laugh and clap!

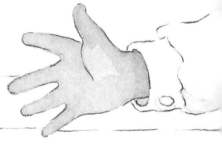

Hooray, I say, I did it!
I'm really glad I tried!
Mom and Dad are happy
and I feel great inside!

Bye-bye, pee! Bye-bye, poop!
I say with a wave and a cheer.

Dad says, "Let's call Grandma.
This is news she'll want to hear!"

It's time to go with Mom and Dad
to buy new underwear.

SPECIAL
UNDERWEAR

Can you guess who gets to choose
that very special pair?

I'm a big girl now!
I can run and jump and play!

I don't want a wet diaper
to get in my way.

Want to know a secret?
You can do it too!

Just march off to the potty
like me and Teddy do.

I'm off to the potty.
No more diapers for me!

And I feel great,
I am proud of...ME!